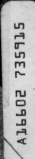

OUTSIDE,

INSIDE

BY Carolyn Crimi

ILLUSTRATED BY

Linnea Asplind Riley

Simon & Schuster Books for Young Readers

SIMON & SCHUSTER BOOKS FOR YOUNG READERS

An imprint of Simon & Schuster Children's Publishing Division

1230 Avenue of the Americas, New York, New York 10020

SIMON & SCHUSTER BOOKS FOR YOUNG READERS

is a trademark of Simon & Schuster. Book design by Paul Zakris.

The text for this book is set in 36-point Wade Sans Light.

The illustrations are made of cut and painted paper.

Manufactured in China

10 9 8 7 6 5 4 3 2 1

Library of Congress Cataloging-in-Publication Data

Crimi, Carolyn.

Outside, inside / by Carolyn Crimi ; illustrated by Linnea Asplind Riley.

p. cm.

Summary: During a storm, Molly notices different things outside her window and inside her house.

[1. Storms—Fiction. 2. Nature—Fiction. 3. Perception—Fiction.]

I. Riley, Linnea Asplind, ill. II. Title.

PZ7.C86928Ou 1995 [E]—dc20 93-46897 CIP AC

ISBN: 0-671-88688-6

To my parents, for all their love and encouragement
—CC

Outside, black clouds
sink down to the bottom
of the sky.

Inside, Molly stretches and yawns in her red flannel robe.

Outside, tree leaves flap in the crying wind.

Inside, Molly's slippers whisper down the hall.

Outside, a worried rabbit darts across the lawn.

Inside, Molly's cat sleeps

beneath the needlepoint

footstool.

Outside, the rain spills
from the clouds,
shussh-wissh,
shussh-wissh,
shussh-wissh.

Inside, the clock ticks

in the hall,

tink-tunk,

tink-tunk,

tink-tunk.

Outside, puddles bubble and churn with the falling rain.

Inside, maple syrup slips down a pancake mountain.

Outside, a slash of lightning scratches the sky.

Inside, a spark streaks

out of the fireplace.

Outside, rain rushes over shiny, wet rocks.

Inside, Molly's cat's-eye marbles skim across the hardwood floor.

Outside, thunder

stomps over the hills

and meadows.

Inside, Molly twirls

on her tiptoes.

Outside, the rain slows down, plop . . . plop . . . plop.

Inside, Molly counts the raindrops rolling down the windowpane.

Outside, the garden oozes
with gloppy, sloshy mud.

Inside, Molly squishes fresh cookie dough between her fingers.

Outside, a sparrow shakes the rain from his feathers.

Inside, Molly's cat arches his back after his morning nap.

Outside, the sun pushes through a crack in the clouds.

Inside, Molly swings the

door open . . .

and lets the outside in!